D1489346

characters created by
lauren child

My
wobbly tooth
must NOT ever
NEVER fall out

PUFFIN

Text based on script written by Samantha Hill

Illustrations from the TV animation

produced by Tiger Aspect

PUFFIN BOOKS
Published by the Penguin Group: London, New York, Australia,
Canada, India, Ireland, New Zealand and South Africa
Penguin Books Ltd, Registered Offices: 80 Strand, London WC2R 0RL, England

puffinbooks.com

First published in Puffin Books 2006
This edition published 2012
001 – 10 9 8 7 6 5 4 3 2 1

I have this little sister Lola.
       She is small and very funny.
This week she got her
            first ever wobbly tooth.

Lola says,
"I do not ever NEVER want
my wobbly tooth to fall out."

Marv says, "When I had my first wobbly tooth,
I nearly swallowed it.
Luckily I was eating a toffee...
and my tooth got stuck in it!"

I say, "Once I headed a football
and my wobbly tooth just flew out
of my mouth!"

"But I do not ever NEVER
want my wobbly tooth
to fall out," says Lola.

Marv says, "Why don't
you want it to fall out?"

"I just need to keep completely
all my teeth," says Lola.

And I say, "Those are just your baby teeth
and they are meant to
get wobbly and fall out.
Then you will get new teeth – and
they are your grown-up ones."

"It's like mooses," I say. "Mooses' antlers
fall off and then they get new ones which are
better and stronger."

"But I am not a moose!
It's my wobbly tooth and
I want to keep it... wobbly," says Lola.

Later Lotta comes over to play with Lola.
"Lola, Lola!"

Lola says,
"What is it, Lotta? What is it?"
And Lotta says,
"My tooth fell out!"

"What did you get?"
says Marv.

"What do you mean, what did you get?" says Lola.
And Lotta says,
"Well, the tooth fairy came and…"
"Who is the tooth fairy?!" says Lola.

"The tooth fairy is the tooth fairy...
    I lost my wobbly tooth, I put it under my pillow,
  and then in the middle of the night
the tooth fairy came and then I got
  a coin," says Lotta.
    "And in the morning
I bought this for
    the farm.
It's a
    chicken!"

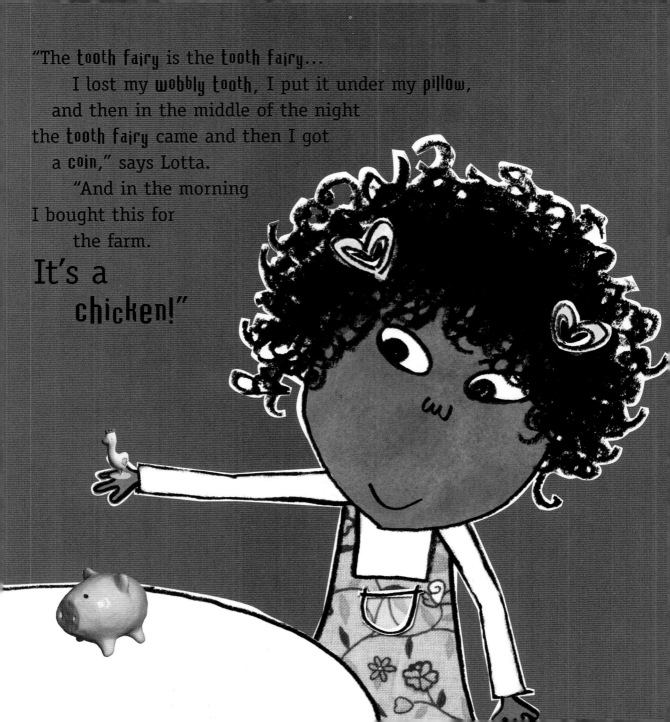

Lola says,
"I didn't know there was a special fairy
who gives you presents when your teeth fall out!
Why didn't somebody tell me this before?

"My wobbly tooth must completely
come out! Now!"

Lotta says,
"When your tooth falls out,
what are you going to get?
We need a horse and a sheep...
and a cow."

And Lola says,
"I'm going to get
a giraffe."

"Do you get giraffes on a farm?"
says Lotta.

And Lola says,
"Yes, you absolutely do, Lotta...

"... but how do I get my wobbly tooth to fall out?"

And Lotta says, "Does it feel wobbly enough?"

Lola says, "I think it's almost nearly
about to come out..."
And Lotta says,
"You have to keep wobbling it."

Marv says,
"Do you want me to twist it?"
"No, Marv!" says Lola. "Mum said
absolutely no twisting!"
And I say, "Keep wobbling, Lola."

"I've been **wobbling** it for ages,"
she says. "It's still
not coming **out**.

I don't think it's **ever**
going to **come out**."

Then she squeals,
"Aaagh!

It's out!
My wobbly tooth
is really out!
And now I can get my giraffe!"

Lotta says,
    "You have to put it under your pillow
in the very, very middle.
        You must go to bed early,
            and you must fall asleep quickly,
or the tooth fairy won't come."

Lola says, "Yes. Because I really want
                    my giraffe."

"I want the **giraffe** too!" says Lotta.

"When you come over tomorrow,"
    says Lola, "I can have my **giraffe**
and you can bring your **chicken**
        and they can be **friends**."

"Yes, **yes**, **yes!**" says Lotta.
    "Bye, Lola!"

At bedtime Lola says,
"Charlie, I'm just going to wash
my **tooth** and make it shiny and clean.
And then I...

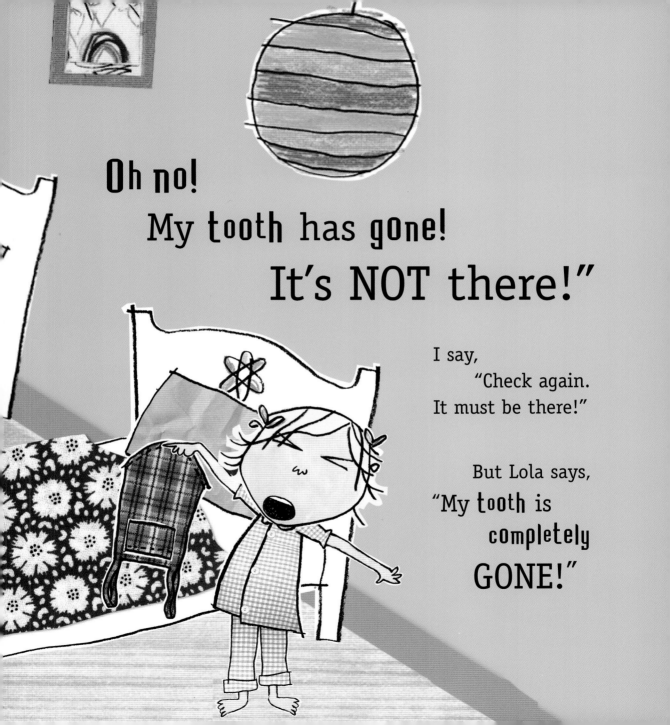

Oh no!
My tooth has gone!
It's NOT there!"

I say,
   "Check again.
It must be there!"

But Lola says,
"My tooth is
      completely
GONE!"

I say,
"It must be somewhere!"

So we
start
searching
everywhere.

We look in the sink,

and

under
the
beds,

on   the   floor,

and

around the sofa.

Everywhere.

Then I have a really good idea.

"If you go to sleep and dream really
happy dreams, you will smile.
And then the tooth fairy will see
the gap in your teeth,
and she'll know you really did
lose your tooth!"

So Lola goes to bed.

"Really happy dreams.
Really happy dreams. Really happy..."

In the morning
Lola looks under the very
middle of her pillow.

She says,

"Charlie! The tooth fairy did come!
Look! Hurry, hurry, Charlie,
I need to get a giraffe!"

When Lotta comes to play with Lola she says,
    "What's your **giraffe** called?"
Lola says, "**Giraffe**. And what about your **chicken**?"
    Lotta says, "It's called **Chicken**!"
"Oh **look**! I think they're **friends**," says Lola.

Then Lola says, "Maybe Giraffe and Chicken
would like to meet Mr Goat?
Oh, we don't have a goat."
"How will we get a goat?" says Lotta.
"We need more wobbly teeth!" says Lola.
"Have you got any more wobbly teeth?"

Lotta says, "No."
"What about this one?" says Lola.
"No," says Lotta.
Lola says, "Try that one.
This one? This one? This one..."